JASON STRANGE

The Mothman's Shadow

Cover Illustration by Serg Soleiman

Interior Illustration by Phil Parks

STONE ARCH BOOKS
a capstone imprint

Jason Strange is published by Stone Arch Books
A Capstone Imprint
151 Good Counsel Drive, P.O. Box 669
Mankato, Minnesota 56002
www.capstonepub.com

Library of Congress Cataloging-in-Publication Data is available on
the Library of Congress website.

Library Binding: 978-1-4342-2965-6
Paperback: 978-1-4342-3093-5

Summary: A camping trip goes horribly wrong for a group of teenage boys.

Art Director/Graphic Designer: Kay Fraser
Production Specialist: Michelle Biedscheid

Photo credits:
Shutterstock: Nikita Rogul (handcuffs, p. 2); Stephen Mulcahey (police badge, p. 2);
B&T Media Group (blank badge, p. 2); Picsfive (coffee stain, pp. 2, 5, 12, 17, 24, 30,
42, 48, 57); Andy Dean Photography (paper, pen, coffee, pp. 2, 66); osov (blank notes,
p. 1); Thomas M Perkins (folder with blank paper, pp. 66, 67); M.E. Mulder (black
electrical tape, pp. 69, 70, 71)

Printed in the United States of America in Stevens Point, Wisconsin.
092010   005934WZS11

TABLE OF CONTENTS

– Chapter 1: **The Long Road** –

The old station wagon tumbled along
Highway 13. Noah Stiles's older brother,
Ben, had only had his drivers' license for a
couple of months. Somehow he'd talked their
parents into letting him borrow the car for
the trip.

"This is scary," Noah's friend Gavin said
from the backseat.

"Relax," Ben said. He glanced quickly
over his shoulder. "I know what I'm doing."

The car swerved hard around a curve. The tires screeched. All the boys jerked back and forth before the car finally straightened out.

"See?" Ben said, chuckling. "No problem. We're fine."

"I didn't mean your driving," Gavin said. "You drive just like my mom."

"So what are you talking about?" Noah asked. He turned halfway around in the passenger seat to look at his friend.

Kyle and Josh were in the way back. One seat was empty. It was supposed to be for Sam, Noah's best friend. That morning, though, when the boys pulled up to Sam's house to pick him up, Sam had run out and said he couldn't go. A family emergency had come up. He'd have to stay home.

Gavin leaned forward. "Are you kidding, Noah?" he said. "Kyle and Josh, back me up here. Aren't you guys all scared . . . of Monday?"

Ben howled with laughter. He shook his head. "Now that makes sense," he said. He looked at Josh and Kyle in the rearview mirror. Then he glanced at his brother, next to him. Noah rolled his eyes and turned away.

"Gavin is smart to be scared," Ben said, nodding. "Freshman year in high school was probably the scariest thing I ever went through."

Ben was going to be a senior starting Monday. He'd been looking forward to it forever, it seemed like. According to Ben, senior year was going to be a cake walk.

"You worry too much," Kyle said. He leaned on the back of his seat. "It'll be fine. What's the worst that could happen?"

"Are you kidding?" Gavin said, stunned. "Here's a list: bad grades, getting lost in the halls between classes, ending up with a mean homeroom teacher . . ."

"Don't forget getting beat up by seniors," Ben added. He sneered at Noah and gave him a punch in the shoulder. "Ha!"

"Quit it," Noah said, rubbing his arm. "That didn't even hurt."

"Don't ask for worse, little brother," Ben said. He nodded at the road ahead. A little sign read "Hidden Lake, 5 miles."

"We're almost there," Noah told his friends. "Five miles to Hidden Lake. We'll be there in a few minutes."

The family cabin was at Hidden Lake, in the hills overlooking the little town of Ravens Pass. Noah and Ben's parents hardly ever talked about it. Noah wasn't sure why. He knew that when his great-great-uncle Jeb died, he left the cabin to them, his only living relatives. But Mom and Dad weren't exactly "back-to-nature" types. Noah's mom went up to the cabin once, to see if it was worth selling. When she got back to the city, she reported that the best plan might be to just burn it down.

Over the years, they'd talked about cleaning it up and selling it, but it never seemed to get done. Now, with only one weekend left of the summer before high school, Noah had convinced his parents to let him and his friends actually use it — as long as Ben was there to look after them.

The road to the cabin was right off the highway, but Ben nearly missed it. It was unmarked and unpaved. At dusk, it was very hard to see.

Ben took a sharp right turn at the last moment, sending gravel and dust up behind him. With the back windows wide open, Josh and Kyle got a mouthful of the stuff.

"Slow down, Ben!" Josh shouted between coughs.

"Sorry," he called back. "The good news is we're here."

The driveway was long and winding. The woods grew thicker and thicker as the station wagon moved slowly down the gravel road.

At one point, the road curved sharply to the left at a break in the woods. The boys got a perfect view of the lake. The car stopped.

"Wow," Gavin said.

The sun was setting on the far side of the lake. Its reflection in the still water was bright orange and purple. The boys sat and stared in awe.

"Um, unless one of you is going to write a poem about this," Ben said, "I'm going to keep driving."

The others laughed, and the station wagon slid down the last fifty feet of driveway to the cabin.

— Chapter 2: **Spooked** —

"This place is a dump," Ben said, standing in the center of the cabin's main room. "Mom was right."

Besides the main room, there was a tiny kitchen, a tinier bathroom, and two small bedrooms. Each room had two bunk beds, so there was room for nine people to sleep if someone slept on the couch.

"It's not so bad," Noah said. He sat on the couch and bounced to test it out. "I like it."

Ben shook his head. "Weirdo," he said. Then he yawned and stretched. "I'm going around back to see how much firewood we have. Then if you babies can handle it, I'll tell you a scary bedtime story."

Gavin plopped down on the couch next to Noah, and Josh and Kyle each sat on the big rug near the fireplace. A draft came in through the open flue, and Noah shivered.

"A fire will be good," he said. "I can't believe how cold it's gotten."

Kyle shrugged. "We're up pretty high in the mountains and only a few feet from the lake," he said. "It's bound to be colder than down in the city, even during the summer."

The boys sat in silence for a few minutes.

"What's taking Ben so long?" Noah said finally. "All he did was go to get firewood."

Josh shrugged. "So go check on him," he said. "I'm too comfortable to get up." Josh leaned back until he was lying flat on the thick rug.

Noah sighed loudly, but got up. He went out the front door and stopped. The night sky was bright with stars, and they shined onto the lake so it looked like there were twice as many: a million in the sky and a million in the water.

"Ben?" he called out. There was no answer. The night was full of quiet sounds, like the hooting of an owl, the gentle ripple of water on the lake, and the breeze through the tall pines all around.

"Ben? Where are you?" Noah called again. A twig snapped nearby, and he spun. "Who's there?"

Noah squinted into the woods, hoping he wouldn't see a skulking figure looking back. "Is that you, Ben?" he said. "Stop goofing around."

A hand grabbed his shoulder, and Noah screamed. "Don't hurt me!" he shouted.

Ben laughed in reply. "Wow, are you a baby," Ben said. "I can't believe how easy you are to scare."

Noah turned around and faced him. Ben was smiling, and under one arm he had a bundle of firewood. "Jerk," Noah said. "What took you so long, anyway?"

Ben shrugged. "I was hoping you'd come looking for me," he said. "And my plan worked perfectly."

He shook his head, still laughing, and went inside the cabin.

– Chapter 3: **Just Stories** –

The boys sat in a circle on the rug in front of the fire. Gavin was in charge of cooking the hot dogs they'd brought. He held them over the flames on a long stick while Ben finished his ghost story.

"A low whistle came from under the bed," Ben said. "So little Jimmy climbed out from under the covers and got down on his knees to look. When he did, a bony hand reached out!"

The boys jumped as Ben threw his hands out, as if to grab their throats. Instead he grabbed his own.

"The hand grabbed Jimmy by the throat and squeezed," Ben went on, pretending to gag. "Soon, Jimmy couldn't breathe. The world went black."

The boys leaned forward, holding their breath, just like Jimmy.

"That's it," Ben said, relaxing and leaning against the couch. "The end."

"That's a dumb ending," Kyle said. "What even happened?"

Gavin got up from the floor and handed out the hot dogs. "I agree," he said. "Lame story, Ben."

"Yeah, lame," Noah said, laughing. He took his hot dog and climbed onto the couch.

He lay on his back and looked at the fan spinning slowly on the ceiling. But he didn't really think the story was lame. In fact, his heart was racing.

"Well, I'm exhausted," Ben said. He got up. "That three-hour drive really does make you tired, just like Dad always says."

Ben slapped his brother on the head. "Good night," he said.

"Ow, quit bugging me," Noah snapped back.

Ben laughed and strolled into one of the bedrooms. Before the door closed, he shouted out, "There are four beds in the other room, which is enough for all you babies. So don't come in here!"

Noah heard the door lock, and he shook his head. "Jerk," he mumbled.

"I'm tired too," Josh said. "If we want to do some fishing tomorrow, we better get some sleep."

Noah checked his watch. It was already after eleven.

The other boys all started for the second bedroom. "Um, I'm going to stay up for a little while," Noah said.

Kyle shrugged. "Suit yourself," he said. Then he closed the door.

Noah closed his eyes. After the scare his brother gave him outside, and that ghost story, he knew he wouldn't be able to sleep for a while.

* * *

Noah was still awake an hour later when he suddenly shivered. He turned his head to look at the fireplace.

The fire, which had been roaring and hot not long ago, was now just a light orange glow. The draft from the flue was back, and Noah wished he had one of the blankets from the bedrooms.

The dying fire made hardly any light. Still, the bright stars, and their light reflecting off the lake, seemed to be enough light. The white curtains over the big front window were lit up by the starlight, so they seemed to glow blue-white.

Noah rolled over again. He curled up facing the back of the couch, with his back to the fire. *I should just go to bed*, he thought. *I should just get up off the couch, walk into the bedroom, and get into bed. I'd probably fall asleep quickly.*

He took a deep breath. Then he froze.

He was sure someone had been looking at him through the thin curtains, lit up with starlight.

You're imagining things, Noah thought. *Just roll over and look at the curtains. Then go to bed.*

In his head, Noah counted: *One, two . . . three.* Then he rolled over. His breath caught in his throat.

In the window, behind the gauzy curtains, was the silhouette of a man. It rose slowly behind the curtains. Noah put his hand over his mouth to stop himself from screaming.

As the figure rose, its shoulders and arms seemed to grow bigger, until at last a pair of huge wings appeared. Now Noah couldn't stop himself. He screamed.

– Chapter 4: **A Nightmare?** –

"What is going on out here?" Ben said as he stumbled out of his bedroom.

Noah was curled up on the couch. He pointed at the window, waving his arm around wildly. "I saw . . . something," he said. "Out there."

"Okay," Ben said. He went over to the window and opened the long curtains. Then he peered out the window. "Anything in particular?"

Noah opened his mouth to talk, but couldn't think of how to tell his brother what he'd seen. Instead, he jumped up from the couch and flicked the light switch next to the front door.

Outside, two spotlights over the grounds flashed on, flooding the area in light.

Noah hurried to the window next to his brother. "There was a man out there," he said. "I think."

Gavin, Kyle, and Josh came out of their room. "What's all the ruckus out here?" Gavin asked.

"Yeah," said Josh. "I'd just fallen asleep and then you start screaming."

"I only screamed once," Noah said, sitting back down on the couch. "Someone was looking in the window. I'm sure of it."

Ben opened the front door and stepped outside. Noah stood behind him. No one could have been hiding in the brightness of the outdoor floodlights.

"I guess he's gone," Noah said.

"Or," Ben said, closing the door, "there was no one there at all." He switched off the floodlights.

"I saw someone," Noah said. "Seriously, guys. I'm sure of it."

Gavin shook his head and went back into the second bedroom. "Good night," he said.

Josh and Kyle shrugged and followed Gavin. "See you in the morning," Kyle said. The door to the second bedroom closed.

Noah sat on the couch and slumped against the arm.

Ben sat next to him and sighed. "You probably just fell asleep," he said. "Forget about it, okay? It was a dream."

Noah shook his head. "I'm so sure I saw it," he said.

"It?" Ben said. "I thought you said it was a man."

"Oh," Noah said. He got up from the couch. "Never mind. I guess I'll get to bed." He started for the second bedroom.

"Your friends are probably sleeping already," Ben said. "You can sleep in my room."

"Thanks," Noah said, and the brothers went into the first bedroom.

Noah's bed was right by the window. He lay there, listening to his brother snore. The blinds were down, but Noah couldn't resist.

He had to look.

Carefully, Noah pushed two slats of the blinds apart and peered through. At first he saw nothing. He smiled a little and took a deep, slow breath.

"Finally," he whispered to himself. "Maybe I can get some sleep."

But just as he let the slats fall back together, something flashed outside. Noah sat up and pulled the blinds wide open. Only a few feet from the window, staring right at Noah, was a tall man with red, shining eyes.

– Chapter 5: **The Police** –

"Wake up!" Noah shouted. He tugged at Ben's arm. "He's out there. Get up!"

Ben jumped up from his bed and switched on the overhead light. "What are you screaming about?"

Noah pointed frantically out the window. "Look! Look outside!"

Ben ran to the window and looked out. "It's too dark," he said. "I don't see anything."

"That's because you turned on the light," Noah said. He quickly switched it off, then ran back to the window. Just then Gavin, Kyle, and Josh came storming into the room.

"There's nothing there," Ben said.

"I am positive this time," Noah said.

"Positive of what?" Gavin said, yawning.

"I saw a man. He was right outside my window, staring at me," Noah said.

Ben scratched his head and sat on the bed. "You just fell asleep again," he said. "It was a bad dream."

"No way," Noah said. "With the way you snore? I couldn't have slept if I wanted to."

"Is that what that noise was?" Josh asked. "I thought someone was using a bulldozer outside."

"Very funny," Ben said. His face went serious. "Listen, Noah. We're in the middle of nowhere here. You have to tell me the truth. If you really saw someone —"

"I did," Noah said firmly.

Ben shrugged. "Okay," he said. "Then I'm calling the cops."

* * *

Half an hour later, Sheriff Kindred pulled off his hat and dropped it onto the couch. He was a tall man with very little hair on his head. What hair he had was too long and very white. It made him look really old, even though his face didn't have one single wrinkle.

"So, you're Noah?" he asked. Noah nodded. "Tell me what you saw," Sheriff Kindred said.

Officer Ryan, a much younger, shorter man, stood near the door next to Ben. The officer had out his pad and pencil, ready to write down everything Noah said.

"Well," Noah said, "first I saw this man outside that window there." He pointed to the big window at the front of the cabin. The sheriff didn't even turn his head, but Officer Ryan scribbled madly in his pad.

"Then, after I got into bed," Noah went on, "I opened the blinds and saw this man staring at me through the window."

"Did you get a look at his face?" the sheriff asked.

Noah thought a moment. "No, it was too dark," he said. "But his eyes . . ."

The sheriff leaned forward. "What about his eyes, son?" he asked.

Noah flinched. The sheriff's thin lips stretched into the slightest smile.

"Go on, Noah," the sheriff said. "Anything you can tell us will be very helpful."

"His eyes were . . . red," Noah said. "I know, it sounds weird."

"Red eyes?" Officer Ryan said, laughing. "Hey, sheriff. You think it's the Mothman?"

Noah didn't get the joke, but Officer Ryan bent over laughing. "Red eyes!" he howled.

The sheriff didn't appreciate the joke at all. He leapt up from the couch and strode over to his officer. "That's enough of that," he snapped.

Officer Ryan stopped laughing at once and put his eyes back on the notebook. "Sorry, sheriff," he said.

The sheriff turned back to Noah and smiled again. "My officer and I will take a look around the grounds," he said. "You boys stay inside."

With that, the two men left the cabin. Ben stood in the doorway, watching.

"What was that all about?" he asked Noah.

Noah shook his head. "No idea," he said. But he was thinking about those wings he'd seen during the night . . . and those shining red eyes.

Ben went back to watching through the open front door.

"I'm going to lie down," Noah said, and Ben nodded without looking at him.

In the bedroom, Noah left the lights off and sat in bed with the blinds open.

He watched Sheriff Kindred and Officer Ryan outside. They shined their flashlights here and there, sometimes stopping and stooping to look at something on the ground.

When the two men were standing just outside his window, they stopped and talked quietly. Noah opened his window just a crack and strained to listen.

"Ryan, what kind of fool are you?" Sheriff Kindred said.

The officer took off his hat and scratched his head. "I didn't think it was a big deal," he said. "It's just an old legend. I was only joking around."

"Joking, huh?" the sheriff said. "These kids are up here without any adults. Do we need them worrying about a flying monster man?"

"Oh, come on," Officer Ryan said. "You don't really believe that legend, do you, sheriff?"

"That's not the point," the sheriff replied. "If the kids do, we'll have a panic on our hands. I've been sheriff around here long enough to have seen it dozens of times before."

"I guess," Officer Ryan said. "It could become a headache if every broken twig and hooting owl has us back up at the cabin on a wild goose chase."

The sheriff nodded. "Exactly," he said. "The kid probably fell asleep and had a nightmare. No need to give him more fuel for that fire."

"But we found those footprints," the officer said. "What if there's a prowler here?"

"What, those size ten boots?" the sheriff said. He pointed at a spot under Noah's window. "Those are the older boy's, I'd bet. Ben, I think his name was."

"Right," Officer Ryan said, looking at his pad. "Benjamin Stiles, full name."

The sheriff put a hand on the officer's shoulder. "Right, him," he said. "The kid mentioned he'd gone around back to get firewood. Those were from his boots, I'm sure."

"If you say so, sheriff," Officer Ryan said. Then the two men walked back toward the front of the cabin.

Noah quickly closed the window and headed for the main room. As the two officers walked in, he said, "So, did you find anything?"

"Not a thing," the sheriff said. "But if you boys hear or see anything unusual, feel free to call us again. Okay?"

"Yes, sheriff," Noah said.

Ben sighed and glared at his little brother. "Thanks for coming out," he said, turning to the two men. He shook the sheriff's hand, then Officer Ryan's. "We're sorry we bothered you. I think my little brother just got shaken up from some ghost stories."

The sheriff laughed. "Next time you're telling ghost stories, you let me know," he said. "I know a few doozies."

Then the two men tipped their hats and left. Noah stood at the front window and watched as their black and white car drove off, down the long driveway and toward the main road.

That night, when Noah finally fell
asleep, he dreamed he was back home in his
backyard. It was very dark, but his baseball
was lost in the bushes. He got down on his
knees to find it, and hundreds of moths
fluttered out of the shrubs and covered him
like quickly falling snow. They fluttered
against his skin. The crawled over him, into
his mouth and nose and ears.

He woke up in the still dark bedroom,
sweating and breathing heavily, and he
shuddered.

– Chapter 6: **Digging Deeper** –

The next day was hot. The boys sat on the dock, their bare feet hanging over the edge.

The only person who wasn't holding a fishing rod was Ben. Instead, he was sipping from a can of soda, and relaxing on the dock, swinging his legs into the water.

"This is the life," he said, letting the warm sunshine fall over his face. "I can't believe we have to go to school on Monday morning."

Josh yawned. "I can't believe how tired I am," he said. "I feel like I got like, an hour of sleep last night." He glared at Noah.

Noah stared out over the lake. "I don't care what that sheriff said," he said. "And I don't care what you guys say. I know what I saw."

"You were dreaming," Ben said without opening his eyes.

"Oh yeah?" Noah said. "What about what I heard the sheriff and that officer talking about outside my window?"

Ben shrugged. The other boys kept quiet too.

"Ha," Noah said. "You have nothing to say to that." But he didn't feel any better. In fact, he was sure that his friends probably just thought he was a liar.

"I'll do some research," he said. "I'll find out as much as I can about the Mothman. Then you'll see."

No one caught any fish that morning, so for lunch they had to go into town for some fast food.

"Bring me back a chicken sandwich or something," Noah said as Ben and the other boys got ready to go.

"You're not coming?" Ben said, shaking his keys.

Noah shrugged. "I'm going to stay here and take a nap," he said. "I didn't get a lot of sleep last night."

Ben looked at him for a long moment. "Okay, whatever you want to do," he finally said. Then he walked out and closed the door.

Noah went to the window and waited until his brother's old station wagon was far down the long driveway. Then he ran to his bag and found his smartphone.

The service up at the lake wasn't very good, and Noah had to wait forever for each page to load. But he was able to learn a lot about the Mothman.

For generations, the mysterious red-eyed monster had been visiting Hidden Lake. The first report was in the local newspaper almost a hundred years ago.

It described the Mothman as a tall, skinny creature that looked like a man. The only difference anyone could be sure of was its huge wings and glowing, red eyes.

"It had to be the Mothman," Noah said to himself. He looked around the empty cabin.

He was all alone, and the Mothman was out in the woods someplace.

Suddenly he wished he'd joined his brother and friends for fast food.

Noah scrolled through his phone's directory and called Sam's cell phone again. There was no answer, just like the last few times he'd tried.

– Chapter 7: **Lost in the Woods** –

Noah's chicken sandwich was cold by the time the others got back, but he ate it anyway. He hadn't realized just how hungry he was.

There was no more excitement that afternoon. The boys spent most of the day lounging around on the dock or taking short swims. It seemed like everyone was having a lot of fun.

Only Noah couldn't enjoy himself.

Instead, he sat on the dock, or on the couch, or on the fallen tree in front of the cabin. He mostly stared off into space and thought about the Mothman.

The boys had dinner quite late, sitting around a big campfire in front of the cabin. From there, they could watch the lake and enjoy their last real night of freedom. The next day, they'd make the long drive back home. The day after that would be school.

"You sure have been quiet today," Josh said.

Noah barely heard him. "Huh?" he said.

"Earth to Noah," Ben said. He tapped his brother in the forehead several times. "Wake up, little brother."

"Sorry," Noah said. "I guess I'm just tired."

"We all are," Gavin said. "Thanks to you and your friend the butterfly man."

The other boys laughed, except Noah. "Mothman," he said. "And he's real. I found a lot of information about him online."

Kyle squinted at Noah from the other side of the fire. "You found stuff online," he said, "so you think Mothman is real? Um, I hate to tell you, buddy. But if you found stuff online, it probably means he's not real!"

The others laughed and nodded.

Josh got to his feet. "I have to pee," he said. "If I'm not back in a five minutes, the Mothman got me."

The others howled at that. Noah just hung his head.

"We'll call an exterminator," Ben said. That made everyone laugh even more.

Josh wandered off into the woods.

"You guys can say whatever you want," Noah said. "I know what I saw."

He picked a hot dog from the ice chest and skewered it with his roasting stick. It cooked quickly over the huge campfire.

When he was halfway through eating the hot dog, he realized it had been pretty quiet since Josh left. "Hey, he's been gone a while," Noah said.

Ben shrugged. "I guess so," he said. "Think the Mothman got him?"

"Shut up, Ben," Noah said. "He doesn't know these woods at all. He might have gotten lost."

"It's true," Kyle said. "Mothman or not, it can be dangerous out here."

Ben sighed. "I'll get the flashlights."

* * *

Ben led the group into the woods. Their flashlight beams cut through the darkness, landing on trunks and pine needles and fallen logs. As the boys moved their flashlights, everything in the deep woods seemed to move.

"I think he went this way," Ben said.

"Why are you whispering?" Gavin asked. But he was whispering, too.

A deep flutter came from overhead. Noah and Ben shone their flashlights into the canopy as an owl landed on a high branch. It blinked and hooted. The boys walked on.

Ben suddenly stopped. He grabbed Noah's wrist. "This is stupid," he said. "What are we so scared of?"

The others looked at him. "Noah has us all freaked out," Gavin said.

"Josh!" Ben called out. "Josh, where are you?"

They stood and waited for his reply, but heard nothing.

"We should check the dock," Kyle said. "He could have fallen into the lake."

Ben nodded, and they hurried off toward the dock. "Josh!" Ben called out as they walked.

Noah pointed his flashlight's beam at the base of the trees. They began to thin as they moved closer to the lake. As his beam moved quickly something flashed at him: two eyes.

"There," he whispered. He pointed into the darkness. "I saw something."

The boys all shined their lights at the spot. It was Josh. He was sitting against a tree trunk, his knees pulled up to his chest, and he was shaking.

"Josh, what are you doing?" Ben said. "Did you forget how to pee?"

He shook his head once and pointed over their heads. "Up there," he stuttered. His voice trembled. "Something was watching me from the trees. It fluttered and flew away just before you showed up."

Ben rolled his eyes. "It was just an owl," he said. "We just saw the same one a minute ago."

The boys stood around Josh in a half circle, shining their flashlights on him.

"It's true, Josh," Gavin said. "Come on. Get up. You're acting insane right now."

Josh looked from one boy to the next. When he got to Noah, he stared. "Noah knows," he said. "Noah saw him, too."

"I —" Noah started to say, but Josh shouted.

"There!" he said, pointing. "Right behind you!"

– Chapter 8: **Easy to Scare** –

The boys spun quickly and pointed their flashlights, flooding the woods with light and shadow.

A figure stood there before them, its arms over its face to shield its eyes. "Ahh!" it screamed. "What are you morons doing?"

"Sam?" Noah said, lowering his flashlight. "Where did you come from?"

The other boys lowered their flashlights, too.

"I just walked all the way up that crazy driveway," Sam said. Over his shoulder was a small overnight bag. In his hand was his own little flashlight. "I had no idea it would be so long!"

"Yeah," Noah said. "We're way up here, aren't we? But I thought you weren't coming."

"The emergency wasn't as bad as we thought it would be," he said. "So I thought I'd surprise you dorks. My brother dropped me off at the bottom of the driveway."

"Well, you showed up at the craziest possible moment," Ben said. "Josh and my idiot brother here think the woods are haunted by a monster."

"The Mothman," Josh said. He got up and joined the other boys. "I saw him."

Noah nodded. "I did too," he said. "I think."

"You think?" a voice said from inside the woods. Sheriff Kindred stepped out of the darkness. He was carrying his hat and put it on as he strode over to the boys.

"Sheriff Kindred?" Ben said. "What are you doing out here? We didn't do anything wrong, did we?"

"Well, that depends," the sheriff said. He looked at Sam. "I couldn't help overhearing this little stunt you played on your friends."

"Stunt?" Sam said.

"Sneaking up on them in the dark just now," the sheriff went on. "I heard them scream and came over to check it out. Imagine how angry I was to hear it was just some punk kid."

"Oh, I didn't mean to," Sam said. He put his hands in front of him. "Honest. I just happened to walk up. Josh was already scared when I got here —"

"And speaking of that," the sheriff said, "when did you get here?"

"Just now," Sam said. "I walked up the driveway two minutes ago."

"It's true, sheriff," Noah said. "Sam couldn't get here with the rest of us because of a family emergency."

Sam nodded, but the sheriff ignored Noah and stepped right up to Sam. He pulled out his handcuffs and jingled them in his hands. "That's not what I think," the sheriff said. "I think he's been here all along, hiding out in the woods and scaring the rest of you. He's been pretending to be the Mothman."

"What?" Ben said. "That's insane."

"Is it?" the sheriff said, staring at Sam.

Sam was dumbstruck. He stared at the sheriff, his mouth open.

"Is that true, Sam?" Noah asked.

It didn't seem like something his friend would do, but he had seen some crazy things that weekend.

And now here Sam was, showing up at the same time that Josh saw the Mothman.

"It's true," the sheriff said. "And I just realized why you look familiar, Sam. You're on a wanted poster back at the precinct, aren't you?"

"What?" Sam said. "Me?"

The sheriff grabbed Sam's wrist and was about to handcuff him.

"Turn off those flashlights, you kids," he said. "You don't want to see what's about to happen."

The other boys obeyed, but exchanged confused glances. Was the sheriff really about to arrest Sam?

Suddenly the sheriff laughed. He looked at Noah and threw his head back. His mouth opened in a huge laugh.

Just as quickly his face went starkly serious. "That's the problem with kids today," he said. He let go of Sam's wrist and put the handcuffs away. "It was never this easy for my father or grandfather."

Noah looked into the sheriff's eyes, and they began to glow.

"But nowadays," the sheriff went on, "you just scare too easily."

His eyes flashed red. Then he raised his arms and two huge, heavy wings sprouted from his shoulders. With a flutter that threw a breeze over the boys, the sheriff rose into the treetops and vanished into the night sky.

Case number: 39592

Date reported: September 2

Crime scene: Hidden Lake, just outside Ravens Pass

Local police: Sheriff Actias Kindred, with the force for 30 years; Officer Jerrod Ryan, a rookie

Civilian witnesses: Noah Stiles, age 13; Ben Stiles, age 16; Gavin Dark, age 13; Kyle Rambow, age 14; Josh Lincoln, age 13, Sam West, age 14

Disturbance: Mothman spotting at a cabin on the lake (old Jeb Stiles's place)

Suspect information: The Mothman is a local menace. He's not harmless. He's dangerous. But once you've discovered his identity, he can't hurt you. At least as far as I know.

CASE NOTES:

I WAS CALLED IN JUST AFTER MIDNIGHT. KINDRED HAD DISAPPEARED. OFFICER RYAN WAS ON THE SCENE, BUT HE WAS A ROOKIE — HE DIDN'T KNOW WHAT HE'D GOTTEN HIMSELF INTO.

THOSE KIDS WERE UPSET. THE MOTHMAN HAD BEEN THERE, RIGHT IN FRONT OF THEM, AND HAD FLOWN AWAY. THEY DIDN'T WANT TO SHOW IT, BUT I COULD TELL THEY WERE FREAKED OUT. I TOLD THEM WHAT I KNOW ABOUT THE MOTHMAN, AND THAT MADE THEM FEEL BETTER, BUT IT WAS A ROUGH NIGHT FOR THOSE BOYS.

KINDRED WON'T SHOW HIS FACE AROUND THESE PARTS AGAIN, THAT MUCH I'M SURE OF. RYAN — WELL, NOW HE'S GOT A STORY TO TELL BACK AT THE STATION. AND THE BOYS? I DOUBT THEY'LL EVER BE THE SAME.

I ORDERED THE STILES PLACE TO BE BURNED TO THE GROUND.

DEAR READER,

THEY ASKED ME TO WRITE ABOUT MYSELF. THE FIRST
THING YOU NEED TO KNOW IS THAT JASON STRANGE IS
NOT MY REAL NAME. IT'S A NAME I'VE TAKEN TO HIDE MY
TRUE IDENTITY AND PROTECT THE PEOPLE I CARE ABOUT.

YOU WOULDN'T BELIEVE THE THINGS I'VE SEEN, WHAT I'VE
WITNESSED. IF PEOPLE KNEW I WAS TELLING THESE STORIES,
SHARING THEM WITH THE WORLD, THEY'D TRY TO GET ME TO
STOP. BUT THESE STORIES NEED TO BE TOLD, AND I'M THE
ONLY ONE WHO CAN TELL THEM.

I CAN'T TELL YOU MANY DETAILS ABOUT MY LIFE. I CAN TELL
YOU I WAS BORN IN A SMALL TOWN AND LIVE IN ONE STILL. I
CAN TELL YOU I WAS A POLICE DETECTIVE HERE FOR TWENTY-
FIVE YEARS BEFORE I RETIRED. I CAN TELL YOU I'M STILL
OUT THERE EVERY DAY AND THAT CRAZY THINGS ARE STILL
HAPPENING.

I'LL LEAVE YOU WITH ONE QUESTION—IS ANY OF THIS TRUE?

JASON STRANGE
RAVENS PASS

Glossary

convinced (kuhn-VINSSD)—made someone agree

dumbstruck (DUM-struhk)—shocked into silence

emergency (i-MUR-juhn-see)—a sudden and dangerous situation that must be dealt with quickly

exterminator (ek-STUR-muh-nate-ur)—a person whose job is to kill pests like bugs or rodents

flue (floo)—a hollow pipe that carries smoke away from a fire

legend (LEJ-uhnd)—a story handed down from earlier times

overlooking (oh-vur-LUK-ing)—looking down on something from above

prowler (PROU-lur)—someone who wants to commit a crime

silhouette (sil-ou-ET)—a dark outline seen against a light background

skulking (SKUHL-king)—sneaking

slats (SLATS)—long, narrow strips of wood or metal

DISCUSSION QUESTIONS

1. Who was the Mothman?

2. What was the scariest part of this book? Why?

3. Did anything happen in this book that made you believe the ending would be different? Talk about it.

WRITING PROMPTS

1. This book is a ghost story. Write your own ghost story.

2. At the end of this book, the sheriff flies into the sky. What happens next? Use your imagination! Write a chapter that extends this book.

3. Pretend you're Noah. Write a letter to a friend about what happened in this book.

for more

Monster
GHOST
secret
JASON STRANG
creature

visit us at www.capstonepub.com